I0521461

Able Publishing
a division of Kent Creative, LLC.

Art: Jared Tuttle, Jared Tuttle Illustration & Design

Fonts: Helvetica, Dennes Old handwriting, Gin (License held at MyFonts.com)

For a FREE study guide to Volume One,
and to be alerted immediately
when Volume Two is complete, go to:

www.KX12Book.com

You can also follow Dan at:
twitter.com/thatdankent

And Proktos has been discovered at:
twitter.com/ProktosPew

To Tom Gams

Thank you for introducing me to both theology and Bob Dylan.

Thank You to my readers:

Barbara Schendel
and
Rosemary Schendel
Jes Brookes
Scott Boren
Marcus Johannes
Valerie Schonewill
Chery Sidler
Asa Tessness

For a FREE study guide, go to:
KX12book.com/studyguide/

PREFACE

I know what you're thinking: *How did a guy like this end up with letters from demons?* Sorry, I'm not telling. There are two reasons for my secrecy: (1) People shouldn't be seeking demons, as seeking demons is just the sort of thing a demon would like us to do. Instead, we should be seeking God. (2) I am not really sure how I acquired them.

In early 2011 I was part of a team commissioned to install a new method of telecommunication deep underground. The machine, which ultimately failed, was intended to transmit wireless data signals through the earth (rather than bouncing them off satellites, which is far more expensive). I was in charge of testing the quality of data transfer at different frequencies.

On April 29th 2011, in western Minnesota, there was an earthquake. It was a feeble quake, registering a mere 2.5 in magnitude. At ground level you could hardly tell it even happened. But deep underground, where our laboratory was, the quake was surprisingly disruptive. I was called down immediately to our control center and found computers, monitors, printers, and tables all over the place, upside down, sideways, with papers everywhere.

The system was still powered down from the day before, but we were, at that moment, somehow receiving loads of strange data. "Where is all this coming from? What frequency?" I asked, but with the monitors blown out there was no way to know. So I began downloading as much of the data as I could on a woefully small portable hard drive. My access was short lived. Maybe the demons caught on to me and switched frequencies, I don't know. I could only fully download a few folders with, maybe, several thousand files. Let me say, judging from various data metrics, there were tens of thousands of folders, full of endless files, I didn't have the opportunity to get.

A few months after the telecommunications project was canceled, I began investigating the files. What I found were thousands of correspondences written in a sloppy mix of academic German and transliterated ancient Hebrew (thank you Dr. Haggler for your invaluable linguistic assistance). A couple years of translation produced the text you find here—a small portion of our overall pull. Of course, at first I thought it was all a hoax. But the sheer volume of files made that hypothesis unlikely.

One should read these texts with caution, keeping in mind they were written by an untrustworthy mind. As you read them you may notice great similarity, both in concept and in strategy, to the remarkable findings of C.S. Lewis in his collection *The Screwtape Letters*. Indeed, that collection could be read as a supplement for this one, as demonic strategy has, apparently, not changed much over the years.

The demons refer to hell as The Corporation, and they are exceedingly fond of acronyms. Due to incredible luck, I happened upon an acronym key among the downloaded files. All acronym translations will therefore be placed in [brackets] by me. The documents are not important in-and-of themselves.

Don't get too caught up in them. But the nature of them, and the number of them, represents an interesting aspect of the culture of these beings.

I chose to present the correspondences in the order of the date stamp on each file. I hope they are enlightening to you. If people find value in them, I will continue translating the remaining files.

Dan Kent

"Let's not let Satan exploit us, for we are not ignorant of his schemes."

2 Corinthians 2:11

CORRESPONDENCE 1

THE NAME

Recipient: KX12
Source: Proktos Pew
Transmission #00022
Prospect Age: 2y 6m 4days

Thank you for the great laugh! Your last correspondence included a request to be given a name. A name! You haven't even secured one measly soul, and you want a name?

Listen, my funny little helper, right now your passion must be to conquer your prospect. Thoroughly. Do remember, KX12, you have been promoted to a great duty. I urge you to treat it with the singularity of focus and totality of effort it deserves. Judging from the sloppy way you completed your PID [Prospect Initiation Document], one would think you didn't care about your new duty at all.

The Corporation is a results-oriented organization. You earn your place by converting prospects. By making sales. Think on that should your attention drift from your prospect to smaller ambitions like your name. From this point forward I expect more pertinent questions. And, unless you have just converted a prospect, I do not care to hear anything about *you*.

Never forget: I am your supervisor. I am not customer service.

Be prudent, KX12. Give your attention to your prospect now, and he will be obliged to give you his attention for all eternity.

But I suppose, if receiving a name is an incentive for you, I should think about it. After all, that is what The Corporation is all about: rewards and punishments, incentives and disincentives. As your superior, of course, I get the honor of choosing your name. So far, I am rather fond of BrainCramp, or ThoughtFog. Of course, it's all moot if you do not start producing results.

Sincerely,

Proktos Pew

Director of Information Dissemination and Outcomes Evaluation, Prospect Acquisition Department

CORRESPONDENCE 2

THE BIOGRAPHER

Recipient: KX12
Source: Proktos Pew
Transmission #00024
Prospect Age: 2y 6m 7days

    I am pleased with the relevance of your inquiry. Your newfound professionalism has been duly noted. However, now that you have decided to take your job more seriously, you seem hysterical. Your writing drips with anxiety. "I can't seem to tempt him," you say, and, "I do not even think he is aware of me," and, "what possible sin can I tempt a toddler with that will have any bearing on his soul."
    Calm down, KX12.
    Give no effort to tempting this boy.
    Now is not the time to be trying to get him to *do* anything. During these long and tedious years, which reek of naive joy and offensive play, your work is primarily to build a thorough understanding of your prospect. Know him deep and wide, KX12. Then, when the time of tempting comes, you will be familiar with every inclination, vulnerability, and emotional tendency of the boy. By then, if you are responsible with your work, you will have a robust strategy to exploit everything you have learned.
    Can I assume you have already been consulting with the associates assigned to his parents? His father is managed brilliantly by Stubnugget. His mother is managed by the distractible, but creative, KX09. Profit off their work as they will certainly profit off of yours.

During these early years you are primarily a biographer, not a tempter. So crouch deep within a sharp shadow, or secure yourself behind a drapery, and establish a good observation point. There will be cuteness and great gaiety, so shield your eyes, plug your nose, and do your work.

Onward!

Sincerely,

Proktos Pew

Director of Information Dissemination and Outcomes Evaluation, Prospect Acquisition Department

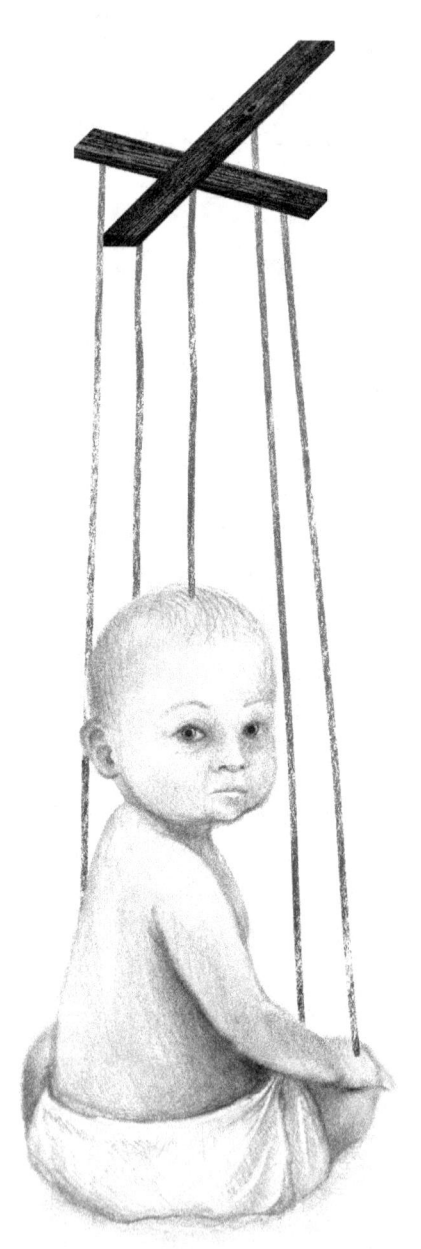

CORRESPONDENCE 3

INNOCENCE

Recipient: KX12
Source: Proktos Pew
Transmission #00067
Prospect Age: 3y 1m 24days

According to your most recent PSR [Prospect Status Report] you are still trying to tempt the boy. Stop that! The enemy designed these prospects in such a way that they maintain an impenetrable cloud of innocence for a good 7 to 10 years. Much of the chaotic and destructive things they do, which appear wicked and devious, are simply the accidental consequences of the boy's clumsiness as he becomes familiar with the complex machinery that is his body, his brain, and his personhood.

Cognitively, he will grow faster than at any other time in his life. You will marvel at how rapidly his brain will develop, and at the furious rate he will begin to comprehend language. It can be overwhelming for a new associate such as yourself.

Morally, though, he will remain numb and unmalleable. This is not to say there is nothing for you to do. Make no mistake, there is no time for dawdling. As I've said before, now is the time for you to understand him thoroughly. And by "understand him" I also mean that you must understand those around him. You need to know which tools you have at your disposal. For instance: the boy's father. Now there is a tool you can use! Stubnugget has done a marvelous job with this dope and we would be fools not to profit off of all his labor.

But father is just one of many tools you have at your disposal. This is why it's so important to be thorough when you fill out your TAR [Toxic Assets Report]. This document captures every corrupted, or converted, individual in your prospect's sphere (uncles, cousins, neighbors, bus drivers, and all other useful people). The pathetic version you sent me had a measly 47 pages! Either you're a fool or you think I am!

Be sure to consider everyone in his geographical region, even if they are not associated with the boy in any way. You just never know. Down the road, at certain times, you may find one of these strangers to be just the perfect person to cross paths with your prospect.

Be creative, KX12. Use the resources all around him.

Your prospect is shrouded from you for a long while yet. You can't get at him directly. But humans can. Other humans can penetrate his cloud of innocence. Due to the tireless work of your fellow associates, the boy is surrounded by abusers, pedophiles, and a breath-taking variety of what a parent might call *bad examples*. Fear not, KX12, his cloud of innocence is perpetually at risk of intrusion.

Sincerely,

Proktos Pew

Director of Information Dissemination and Outcomes Evaluation, Prospect Acquisition Department

CORRESPONDENCE 4

DISRUPTION

Recipient: KX12
Source: Proktos Pew
Transmission #00072
Prospect Age: 3y 6m 23days

Truly innovative organizations are disruptive organizations.

And when it comes to disruption, you will find, The Corporation excels. We *must* be disruptive, or we lose. The simple reason for this: the enemy is the architect of the marketplace. He designed the battlefield upon which we fight. Everything has intended purposes. Night time for sleeping, food for eating, water for drinking, coitus for bonding and procreation. Things like that.

Done within the constraints of their intended purpose, these activities produce benefit and a certain level of pleasure for prospects. Regrettably, should a prospect learn to live within these constraints, they become nearly impossible to convert. This is why we must work so hard at disrupting these intended purposes. We must get them to do these things for *other* reasons. We must get them to add meanings to common activities, meanings that were never meant to be there.

Take eating, for instance. All that eating really is, at its most basic level, is the nourishing of one's body. That's it. But even this dumb-basic understanding can be greatly disrupted. In fact, Stubnugget and KX09 have done a splendid job of adding all sorts of meaning to eating in the minds of mom and dad.

Eating means all sorts of crazy things to them! Your job is to help your prospect appropriate all of those absurd meanings into his own understanding.

Remember dinner on Wednesday? Your prospect sat with his ham, peas, and carrots. He doesn't care too much for peas, does he? Meanwhile, mom pushes this crazy notion that eating everything on one's plate somehow accomplishes some great thing, that there is something good, biologically and morally, about the act. Remember how our boy writhed to get out of his high chair? And his desperation to get back to his toys? Remember how mommy repeated the same chorus over-and-over: "Finish everything on your plate first, honey"? How painfully he struggled to eat those peas! And when he finally choked down that last heinous orb, mom flooded him with affirmations: "What a good boy you are!" She even got daddy involved in the praise-orgy: "Dad, look what our little guy did. He ate it all!" Then dad chimed in: "That's good work, buddy."

Your prospect stared blankly at all the ridiculous praise. This was your fault. You let a profitable opportunity slip right through your fingers. I'm surprised Stubnugget and KX09 didn't file a complaint.

Focus! Help your prospect convert his parents' ridiculous notions of eating into his own understanding. You might assume this a difficult task, but it's not. In fact, once you get the hang of it, it's simple.

For starters, help him actually feel like a *good*

boy who has done something truly special by simply eating the entire arbitrary amount of food on his plate. When he gorges himself, coerce him to think this is, somehow, an impressive accomplishment. Encourage him to bathe in that strange praise. Help him to process it all and make it his own.

When he does this, when he feels like a good boy simply for eating, then you have gained a powerful foothold in him. Eating will now be about a great deal more than simply nourishing himself, but will now be about: being a good boy. And not just eating, but eating *more*. Eating it *all*. These details matter. If you can get him to buy into such ridiculous ideas at this young age, he will accept it and never challenge the logic of it when he develops the capacity for logic.

At this stage in his life, opportunity for disruption abounds.

He is going to his grandparent's house this weekend. I just know Grandma will totally reinforce his new perverted notion of eating. In fact, she will add dimensions to it. Watch for it. She will say, "Eat up! You can't have any pie unless you finish everything on your plate." Now, if you do your job right, your prospect will begin to associate over-satiation as deserving of a reward! In this way, in these early years, we lay the conceptual framework of his future gluttony.

He'll eat so much he'll be afraid to burp!

And, if Fickle Bell can stop chasing his own tail for a moment, we might even get Grandpa to make a contribution. Grandpa has been known to advise his children, in times of half-finished meals, "There are children in Africa starving who would kill for some eggplant and Brussels sprouts." This would be splendid as food can now also be about fighting starvation for unknown people in far away places.

Imagine the long term opportunities all this will afford you down the road, KX12! Getting him to feel like a good boy for doing such a silly, self-destructive thing as overeating sets him up to self-medicate with food (it always makes him feel like a good boy!). Plus, consider the abuse his body will take as he gorges himself, regularly, the rest of his life. But, most importantly, the more he eats for reasons other than nourishing himself, the less he will listen to his own body. His body will tell him, "I'm full," and, "Stop eating now." But his mind will tell him, "Good boys eat everything." Eventually, he will barely hear his body at all.

How deliciously powerful this plate of food has become! So much disruption just in how he understands eating—we haven't even begun to leverage the *pleasure* of eating yet! The more we can disrupt his understanding of eating the more we will reap ongoing profits for years to come. And eating is just one example. His life, you will find, will be full of opportunities for disruption.

Disrupt them all, KX12! Disrupt them all!

Oh, and document, document, document.

Sincerely,
Proktos Pew

Director of Information Dissemination and Outcomes Evaluation, Prospect Acquisition Department

CORRESPONDENCE 5

SELFISHNESS

Recipient: KX12
Source: Proktos Pew
Transmission #00107
Prospect Age: 3y 7m 2days

Stop embarrassing yourself with your enthusiasm over his insignificant acts of selfishness. The little snot can barely cross the room without falling over or leaking fluids. His behavior still means nothing at this point.

You have to understand that even those bratty acts, which look wholly self-centered and appear to be in our favor, are not really the sort of thing we desire. Not at this age. In fact, they can be disastrous for us. When a young prospect acts in blatantly self-centered ways, they are more often than not simply becoming acquainted with that abstract distinction between themselves and the world around them. They're discovering that part of reality which is them and distinguishing it from that part which is not them.

For us his bratty selfishness is a fragile and threatening state of affairs. Of course, the child could be developing deep habits of selfishness, which plays in our favor. But, more often than not, he's simply developing the dangerous skill of *possessing* things. This is dreadful. Only when the child learns to possess things can they truly give them away, in any meaningful sense. A child can't really give something away that was never theirs to begin with.

Our enemy desires his little ones to be

oppositional. To stomp their feet and shout "No!" But what we want are good little boys and girls. We want these smelly little things to obey their parents without fuss or question. We want them to mindlessly share their toys with other children, and to soak in the approving glow of mommy and daddy. The enemy wants his little ones to hoard things for themselves, see? Not forever, but at least until the child reaches that internal tipping point where they actually feel like they have possessed it—when they genuinely feel like "the toy is mine."

So it is to our advantage, in childhood, that the boy be an obedient little angel, who never questions, who never possesses, and who never stands his ground. *That* is a prospect who will ripen nicely in adolescence, be easy to manipulate in adulthood, and will ultimately be a great laborer for The Corporation.

Sincerely,

Proktos Pew

Director of Information Dissemination and Outcomes Evaluation, Prospect Acquisition Department

CORRESPONDENCE 6

THE SAUCE

Recipient: KX12
Source: Proktos Pew
Transmission #00119
Prospect Age: 4y 2m 17days

Stop whining.

"It's not fair," you say, and, "I'm playing against a stacked deck." Yes the deck is unfairly stacked, but take heart, KX12, the deck is stacked in our favor. You see, we have *The Sauce*, which gives *us* the unfair advantage. The Sauce is a power in the marketplace, in the prospect's own world, initiated long ago by our great Leader, which has evolved into an awesome advantage—a perpetual downward inertia. On its own, The Sauce draws a constant bounty of souls into our great organization. Really, The Sauce will do much of your work for you.

Just look at the world our prospect has been born into. It looks so serene, doesn't it? So organic. So harmless. But in reality his world is a machine—our machine—and every useful prospect becomes a cog. The machine will nudge and prod the boy into just that state of mind that is most conducive to our purposes: self-centeredness.

That's what The Sauce is. A breathtaking system of self-centeredness that hums deep and inconspicuous all around him, making it so easy for him to march along to its melody. He won't even know he's marching. The Sauce will marinate our prospect from every angle. I see it enclosing on him already. You must learn to see this, too. Watch the little chub on the carpet stacking his blocks or coloring his books. His mother and father watch the news where a melodramatic newscaster informs the anxious audience of one tragedy after another. Your prospect is too young to understand the tragedies, but he understands his mother's wide-eyed shock and her silent gasp. He understands his father's hands cupped over his mustache, and that slight, dreadful shaking of his father's head. He understands that bad things are happening just outside his door and not far past his front yard.

Our pudgy little prospect will continue to gather clues and uncover the horrible truth: *he is not safe.* His investigation has already begun. In his mind he already questions: *why must we have so many locks on our door? Why must I be belted to the seat when we drive?* As he ages he will gather more clues. He will hear it on the radio and see it on the news. He will learn that, on any given day, a tornado could tear through his town and destroy him. A furnace malfunction could poison him while he sleeps. Heavens, a comet fragment could scream mercilessly from the sky crushing his blonde little head. He will learn of a truly dazzling array of biological dangers as well: cancers, viruses, flesh-eating funguses [sic], toxins.

Don't count on these fears causing total paralysis, or anything grandiose like that. There remains just enough security, and just enough joy, in his world to counter-balance most of these things. Also, he is just a child. Children struggle to comprehend mortality just as adults struggle to comprehend immortality (if you do your job right).

What The Sauce mostly provides is a sort of persistent apprehension. A chronic hesitation. A mild dread that will tug at his thoughts, reminding him of horrible possibilities and filling his imagination with terrible images. The Sauce fills him with pause. It will encourage passivity and nurture complacency.

This fear of suffering and death is the main ingredient in The Sauce. The second most important ingredient is limitation. Limitation (be it limitation of time, money, land, life, or any other resource) pushes everything in our direction, KX12. He has already felt limitation's nudge. I assume you observed his perplexed expression when he was at the birthday party on Saturday? In the toy room? Did you notice his inquisitive look? I guarantee you he was pondering why little Billy Kendell had so many toys and such a big house while his own house is so much smaller and filled with far fewer toys. You see? Do you see how The Sauce kneads them into asking the right questions? Fills them with perceived deficit? Stokes their sense of entitlement? The Sauce nudges them along, and the prospects plant their own seeds! You simply need to keep those seeds watered.

Help your prospect focus on the arbitrary variations in what other people possess. You will marvel, KX12, at the violence and great moral compromises these idiots will make just to get what they perceive as *their share*. The reality of limitation, more than anything else, compels them—practically forces them—to get as much as they can (because there is only so much) as fast as they can (because death is ever-threatening). It's no wonder survival-of-the-fittest philosophies have served us so well over the years.

I once had a prospect, we promoted him all the way up to Head of Product Development at this large technology company. The company was about to launch a new product (some sort of portable music device), so the corporate hotshots met to establish a price for the product. Someone asked him, "What price-point should we start at?" My prospect made the embarrassing mistake of saying, "I'm not sure. What's it worth?" To my prospect's delight, the board thought he was kidding and laughed hysterically for a good minute or so. In a world drenched in The Sauce, soaked in limitation, you don't ask what a product is worth. What my prospect meant to ask was, "How much can we get?"

The pinch of limitation and the threat of death will bully our boy more than anything. But still, suppose the little booger manages to escape these physical and biological risks, and suppose he manages to avoid poverty, or even becomes filthy rich. Let him! It matters little to us, for he must still contend with the third ingredient of The Sauce: the pressure of personhood.

Here he must contend with our dazzling bounty of psychological products and social programs. Pay close attention to how he reacts to people and events.

There, in his reactions, you can best estimate which psychology products might be most effective for him. Does his skin redden and his brow furl when he doesn't get what he wants? Help him explore the features and benefits of our anger products. Does he seem sensitive to the facial expressions of others? Get him to test our social anxiety products.

Get him to be emotionally reactive now, and when he is old enough to enter society, when he gets out into the world, the poor dope will learn that he is just a fragile piñata for an insane and violent crowd (a crowd that profits at his expense). As he samples our products he will discover a million reasons why he is not good enough, and a million reasons why he doesn't belong. He will discover that he is merely a volatile little commodity in an unstable economy of acceptance and rejection.

You must learn to see all these ingredients and mix them thoroughly into your prospect's life, to both soften him and harden him in all the right ways. The Sauce is all around him, in every place he goes, on every person he meets, in everything he reads, and on everything he sees.

Little-by-little, beneath his awareness, he will give in, becoming evermore self-centered, harassed, and then helpless. He lives his life on a tottering stage, and The Sauce thrusts and pulls him into unstable places. He'll flail and struggle, which will simply work him deeper into his instability.

In this world, that so strongly compels self-centeredness, the enemy actually expects the boy to develop concern for others! In a world that compels self-accumulation, Love-Breath expects self-sacrifice. *He* is the one playing against a stacked deck. He's a naive idealist through-and-through. For your prospect to become other-oriented and self-sacrificial, the boy must do so with extraordinary effort against the powerful gravity of our great machine.

Indeed, the whole game is bent in *our* favor (which is why The Corporation so greatly punishes failure). If you paid any attention in your theology classes you would be rejoicing right now instead of pestering me with your knee-jerk, clueless yammering.

Sincerely,
Proktos Pew

Director of Information Dissemination and Outcomes Evaluation, Prospect Acquisition Department

CORRESPONDENCE 7

TALES FROM THE SAUCE

Recipient: KX12
Source: Proktos Pew
Transmission #00120
Prospect Age: 4y 2m 29days

You asked: *How can I use The Sauce to my advantage?* This question pleases me. Leveraging The Sauce (our system of self-centeredness) against the prospect accounts for most of your work as a sales associate. The Sauce is rich and deep, subtle and complex. At his age, trying to work The Sauce into him directly will fail. You must let him ripen first.

Watch how The Sauce affects his mother, though, how it encourages her to neglect your prospect. Every hour of the woman's day is fraught with Sauce. Ambition pushes her around like a bulldozer. She strives for gain. She is thrust along, trying to get her share, trying to get as much as she can (because there is only so much) as fast as she can (because life is so brief).

Remember Tuesday when the boy was on the swing set and mom was mowing the lawn? (According to KX09's charting, mom was worried about what her neighbors would think if her lawn looked unkempt.) Not only was she mowing the lawn, she was also listening to an audiobook on real estate investing (according to KX09, mom hopes her real estate career will allow her to "be her own boss"). The audiobook teaches agents the subtle art of getting larger fees from their clients (another way of saying "taking more" from others).

The Sauce stresses her. There are only so many hours in the day! Anxiety vibrates through her like a bell. She has developed a habit of binging on unhealthy foods. But she has also been taught by The Sauce that a successful person is peaceful and healthy, so she has a rigid routine of yoga and exercise, requiring a complicated schedule with her husband so that the boy is always looked after.

You know what else a successful person has (according to beer commercials)? "Healthy friendships," by which she vaguely understands to mean wild and raucous acquaintances. So, in exhausted obedience, she has regularly scheduled "girls nights" where she pushes through her fatigue, puts on an air of vitality, exaggerates how wonderful her life is, and pretends to have more fun than she really has.

Like other parents deep in The Sauce, she tries to "fit a child in" to her life, just like she tries to fit yoga in. But the boy isn't just another thing in her day-to-day, is it? No! It lives and breathes, and has its own will and agenda. She tries to wrestle the boy into her schedule, but he fails to comply. And she gets so very frustrated, doesn't she? Recall how angry she became when the little thing kept pestering her to push him on the swing. She threw her headphones into the grass, stomped over to the dangling nuisance, then half-heartedly shoved him a few times. The whole scene was comical in its joylessness. Frazzled mom pushing cheerless boy on swing. What a hoot.

The Sauce causes them to sabotage their own

lives. Remember when mom was trying to talk on the phone to her parents, while studying for her real estate exam, and prospect was coloring airplanes? He thought it would be fun to fly the planes around the kitchen table where mom was sitting. Oh how irritating those airplane noises were as he ran around her with those ferocious, two-dimensional aircrafts! "Why can't you calm down and focus on something!" She forced him into a chair and shoved a crayon into his hand—hilariously ignorant of her own inability to calm down or focus on anything.

So, while your prospect has only barely tasted The Sauce, his parents are soaked in it. In this Sauce-laden life of hers, mom is like a girl jumping rope. She's always moving, and something is always happening, but ...nothing important (except that she is distracted from critical tasks, like being with her boy).

Onward!

Sincerely,

Proktos Pew

Director of Information Dissemination and Outcomes Evaluation, Prospect Acquisition Department

CORRESPONDENCE 8

SELF-CARE

Recipient: KX12
Source: Proktos Pew
Transmission #00133
Prospect Age: 4y 8m 7days

What am I, your professor? Stop frittering away my time with your pointless theology questions. I am here to help you convert a prospect, not to help you have a deep thought.

Also, watch yourself. This question: "How can The Corporation expect to win if the enemy is the ultimate source, creator, and sustainer of the marketplace?" is borderline heresy and has been escalated to the Director of Rule Enforcement and Heresy Remediation.

Don't get me wrong. I might be inclined to kick some theology around with you if you were caught up on your work. But you are woefully behind.

First and foremost, you haven't committed the boy to an emotion program yet. How many times do I need to remind you of this task? The earlier we get the boy committed to that perfect emotion, the one that is perfect for him, the easier it will be later on in his life to convince him that it is not merely an emotion but, rather, part of his identity. "It's just who I am," he will say.

It's time to press him on this.

Also, you are six days behind on your SCACs [Self-Care Assessment Charts]. These charts are crucial. You should be charting how much your prospect sleeps, what he eats, how much water he drinks, how he feels about brushing his teeth, what his work ethic is shaping up to be, and—well, you know good-and-well how to fill out the charts. Do it!

How prospects care for themselves determines what possible tactics we can employ later on. How they treat themselves is practically the whole battle.

Did you see the shoddy job he did brushing his teeth last night? The little sneak barely rubbed three teeth with his brush. This is splendid. Keep encouraging this. It will pay wonderful dividends, if you play it right.

How? In many ways. Here are three that immediately come to mind:

First, he will get cavities when he gets older. This is good because prospects are most often won over by an accumulation of small nuisances rather than any single major life crisis. A person's boat is more often sunk by a million raindrops than by a wave. The less he cares for himself now, the more nuisances we can anticipate later on. Do I have to remind you that the work you are doing now will affect your work when your prospect is at his PCA [Prime Conversion Age]?

Second, his lazy brushing will have no immediate negative consequences. You can play this to your advantage by convincing him that he is "resistant to cavities," and that his teeth are "not like others' teeth." You will be amazed at how easy it is to make these creatures feel invulnerable (even superhuman when you get the knack of it). And I assume you already know how easily these feelings of invulnerability can be massaged into feelings of superiority, right? I don't have to tell you how much easier our work becomes when the prospect develops feelings of superiority, do I?

Third, his lazy brushing represents the beginning of a great relationship with authority. He knew good and well what mommy meant by "brush your teeth," but he discovered just how powerless she is to hold him accountable to these expectations. Keep developing this notion of authority as an inconvenience to be circumvented.

And, document, document, document!

Sincerely,

Proktos Pew

Director of Information Dissemination and Outcomes Evaluation, Prospect Acquisition Department

CORRESPONDENCE 9

PREDICTIONS

Recipient: KX12
Source: Proktos Pew
Transmission #00141
Prospect Age: 4y 11m 1days

Before responding to your inquiry I must first attend to business. You have two weeks worth of PARs [Prediction Analysis Reports] due. Do not minimize the importance of these reports. As you should be painfully aware by now, we're blocked from the boy's brain. What goes on in there, we can't be certain.

I know how frustrating this is.

Your only hope is through constructing hypotheses, testing them, and analyzing the results. We test hypotheses by making predictions about what we think the prospect will do. Without documenting this in great detail you will never improve at making predictions. And if you remain lousy at making predictions (which you are without a doubt the lousiest I have seen), then you have no hope in strategy, and no hope in contingency planning. Document, document, document.

Also, the reports serve as an effective way to review your performance. Sometimes it can be difficult to distinguish what actually causes prospects to buy in to The Corporation: our sales associates (you), or simply the already established downward inertia of the marketplace (The Sauce).

Your most recent fret is that your prospect keeps surprising you by his actions. Or, more bluntly, your predictions suck (could it be that you are avoiding your PARs because you are afraid of revealing how incompetent you are at prediction? It won't work. We all know you are incompetent. Fill out the reports!).

The truth is, under my wise leadership, your understanding of your prospect has improved. You are demonstrating occasional insight. Don't go patting yourself on the back, though. As is often the case with new tempters, your focus remains too narrow. To really understand your prospect you must also understand his most intimate circle of influence. You must especially understand his parents—what motivates them, what exasperates them, and, most important, what are the exploitable flaws in their parenting style.

I implore you to develop a good working relationship with Stubnugget and KX09. Keep in close contact with them and keep up on all of their charting. Your ignorance about your prospect's parents is what led to your most recent prediction failure.

Sincerely,

Proktos Pew

Director of Information Dissemination and Outcomes Evaluation, Prospect Acquisition Department

CORRESPONDENCE 10

FEAR

Recipient: KX12
Source: Proktos Pew
Transmission #00144
Prospect Age: 4y 11m 20days

Why is it each new batch of you fiends seem twice as dumb as the previous batch? I was stunned when I read your TPS report [Tactical Prospect Strategy]. It was idiotic, to say the least. I had to sit down to read it because my mind could barely process the depth of its stupidity. Did you put any actual thought into it? Any at all?

Yes, the world is scary and there are many things your prospect will fear. And, yes, you need to use all of this to your advantage, just as I have been teaching. Yet somehow, according to your TPS, you interpreted this to mean that you should try to make all these scary things actually happen to your prospect.

No!

I didn't think you were that dumb at first. But, sure enough, there you were on Sunday afternoon in a comical fit of malevolent multi-tasking, trying to convince the boy to eat paint chips *and* to wander in to the street, all while you were trying to distract that driver ...Oh, KX12, what a daffy sight!

I understand your logic—well, logic is too great a word for what your head was doing. Rather, your thought must have been something like: *the more bad things that happen to my prospect the better.*

Open your eyes, KX12. Fear is your real power,

not misfortune. Humans handle disaster better than they handle dread. Work the boy into a state of constant fear and you'll find great success. Allow him to experience a real crisis, and you will find great spiritual danger.

In this world, plenty of bad things will happen to him as part of the natural course of life. The Corporation rarely causes any of these bad things to happen, just as the enemy rarely prevents them (for as much as these rattle-brains pray for the enemy to protect them, he is most often content to let them experience life as it is).

In fact, we often try to prevent bad things from happening *more* than the enemy does! We do not want him to experience real suffering until that suffering is most advantageous to us. What we want most of all is to nurture distraction and powerlessness. Let him always feel at risk. Fear makes him feel foggy and needy, which makes him vulnerable to all of our life-coaching programs. And since his attention will be spent on things he can do nothing about (that is, *what will happen to me?*), he will simultaneously be cultivating a sense of powerlessness.

Suffering usually produces the opposite of what we want. Actual suffering often empowers people, as it exposes the actual size of the thing feared. The syringe doesn't hurt as bad as he thinks it will. Being rejected by the beautiful girl doesn't kill him like he thought it would. When he gives a presentation in class, in front of all his peers, he finds it "wasn't so bad after all." More often than not, they learn they can handle their suffering more aptly than they feared. They most often emerge feeling stronger. They see reality more clearly for what it actually is. It is so very difficult to get them to buy into most of our offerings when they feel powerful and are clear in thought. Our whole marketing strategy is designed for a distracted customer base. For needy, powerless people with a distorted impression of reality.

Worst of all, suffering is a love-magnet that rejiggers the mindset of everyone around him in a truly terrifying way. This is especially true of children. You inflict suffering on a child and people will flock to him, flaunting a wide variety of the enemy's corrosive talents: compassion, empathy, servitude, encouragement, hope, GAG! The boy will feel loved, KX12! He will feel understood and cared for! Disastrous! We want him to feel unloved, misunderstood, and alone!

Yes, there may be times when causing suffering and orchestrating adverse events can be advantageous. But it is very dangerous and can sabotage your whole campaign, and you are not yet ready to understand such advanced tactics. Until then, keep the prospect as far away from suffering as you can, while also methodically stoking his fear of it.

I'm issuing an order for you to read Grandmaster Screwtape's 8 volume series on fear-management. I expect a RIP [Reading Integration Plan] completed for each volume. Have that done by week's end.

Sincerely,

Proktos Pew

Director of Information Dissemination and Outcomes Evaluation, Prospect Acquisition Department

CORRESPONDENCE 11

THE PERFECT EMOTION

Recipient: KX12
Source: Proktos Pew
Transmission #00147
Prospect Age: 4y 11m 29days

Just what, may I ask, were you thinking while he was at the daycare center Tuesday? I don't get it. Last week you were obsessed with causing as much suffering to your prospect as possible, now it seems like you're trying to get your prospect to feel as many negative emotions as possible—as if quantity were somehow important!

Butterfly barf!

You're either being foolish or lazy. Or both.

Please understand, it doesn't matter how *many* negative emotions he feels. What we need is for him to feel that *one perfect emotion*. The one that, while being a thorny burden to him, he also, in some sense, takes great comfort in.

The enemy wants him to be a *master* of his emotions. We want him to be a *specialist* of one emotion. The enemy wants him to understand his emotions through the lens of a greater reality. We want him to understand greater reality through the lens of one cherished emotion. You see the difference? We want a connoisseur of one bittersweet feeling, an emotion perverted to his unique temperament.

Let me dumb it down for you. Let's say the emotion is anger. We want him to have a thorough familiarity of the deep and complicated variations of his anger. We want that emotion to burn hotter and deeper than it ought to. Bring him to wallow in the anger. To hate it. Yet also to get drunk off it and to take strange comfort in it. We want him to treasure that emotion so dearly that he will, subconsciously, try to create situations with which to feel it, while at the same time lament it hysterically.

Pay attention. Anger may not be right for your prospect, so don't go running off trying to make him mad. My point is, you need to find the one emotion that fits *him* best, and then hone your focus on that.

The right emotion will be easy to spot once you know how to look for it. From what I see, I would introduce him to one of our self-pity programs. Just watch how all of his negative emotions, even now, convert to a form of self-pity.

Remember Sunday evening when his mother wouldn't let him stay up late to watch the television? He fumed with a red-faced anger and tossed his puzzle. Do you recall how, a few minutes later when he was alone in his room, his anger had transformed into hot sorrow and he appeared to be contemplating how unloved he was? This is a splendid development. He is already steering his emotional ship away from certain emotions and towards other preferred ones. Keep a very close eye on these tendencies.

Humans are deeply vulnerable when it comes to their emotions—don't underestimate their power (believe me, the enemy doesn't). I've seen entire lives secured for us simply because the prospect couldn't let go of an emotion. I had one lady who defined her entire life by a tenacious resentment. To this particular prospect, her resentment justified her loneliness, her drinking, and her career failure. And what did she resent? What was the great injustice that constrained her whole entire life? Simply that her husband left her for another woman.

Now, listen, the enemy is keenly aware of your prospect's emotional vulnerabilities and will fight tenaciously at this intersection. Watch carefully and always be on guard.

Onward!

Sincerely,

Proktos Pew

Director of Information Dissemination and Outcomes Evaluation, Prospect Acquisition Department

CORRESPONDENCE 12

CONCEALMENT

Recipient: KX12
Source: Proktos Pew
Transmission #00157
Prospect Age: 5y 2m 2days

No!

Do NOT, unless given explicit orders from below, reveal yourself to your prospect. Yes, you would certainly scare the piss out of him if you did, but you would also be falling on your own sword in the process.

In the old days we did reveal ourselves to our prospects. But we found this to be too expensive. Sure, when we revealed ourselves we could actively manipulate them, frustrate them, and terrify them. But in doing so we also made spiritual reality obvious. Undeniable. And when they saw us even the dumbest prospects immediately assumed the existence of our enemy. This put us in an immediate marketing disadvantage.

Believe me, it was hard work back then. True, there were more of us, but the work was harder. That is, until our brilliant commander implemented The Great Campaign, which changed the game forever. Basically, the campaign introduced humans to the intellectual comforts of measurement, thereby making anything unmeasurable feel unreal. Uncomfortable.

Humans love measurement. They lust after it. Once they taste it, they long for it. Anything that can be seen, touched, or toyed with takes prominence over anything else. To them, if it can't be seen or measured, it doesn't exist. So, if they don't see us, we don't exist.

This paradigm-shifting strategy, initiated by our cunning leader, essentially cut humanity's evidence base in half, thereby greatly reducing the scope of reality humans believe they can *know*. Today, they only take serious [sic] those things which they can perceive in a controlled manner, narrowing humanity's range of inquiry to only matter. And the gut-busting irony of all this is that we called the movement *The Enlightenment*.

This brilliant move turned our whole corporation around. Conversions jumped immediately and have remained high ever since. True, even within the constraints of measurable reality the enemy is still detectable. After all, the world reeks of design and intention. And when prospects do find the enemy they tend to have a stronger, deeper bond with him. But let the enemy care about prospect quality. We'll take quantity over quality all day long. And, KX12, our quantity has been very good for a very long time.

Of course, we've had lazy, impatient sales associates, like yourself, try to take short-cuts by revealing themselves to their prospects. Believe me, these foolish tempters were greatly punished for their short-sightedness. I'll have PRO [Punishment Records Office] send you the excruciating details of the consequences to dissuade you from any possible foolishness. If your urges to cause this sort of mayhem continue, try inducing a night terror in the boy, or tap into his still shallow subconscious and stoke a nightmare.

Do. Not. Reveal. Yourself.

Also, you are falling further behind on your PARs [Prediction Analysis Reports]. Get caught up immediately.

Sincerely,

Proktos Pew

Director of Information Dissemination and Outcomes Evaluation, Prospect Acquisition Department

THE FIRST CITATION

Recipient: KX12
Source: Thief Squeak
Citation #904-KX-2182744-J7 6964-URA4

Violation:

Sales associate *KX12* made the following comment to Director of Information Dissemination and Outcomes Evaluation, Proktos Pew:

"…and after all of my tedious work I think I have finally pinned down the right emotion program for little **Chase Russel Myers**. *I think he will do best with a robust Self-Pity program. Poor* **Chase** *won't even see…"*

Violated Statute:

18,626.59 b:

"Sales associates will, under no circumstance, use the earthly name of their own prospect in any context, be it in dialogue with peers or superiors. Sales associate may only use prospect's name in documents and logs as quotations of other prospects making reference to primary prospect."

Informant:

Proktos Pew (Director of Information Dissemination and Outcomes Evaluation, Prospect Acquisition Department) informed this office of aforementioned violation and shall hereby be cleared of any collateral punishment.

Sincerely,

Thief Squeak,

Director of Rule Enforcement and Heresy Remediation, Prospect Acquisition Department

CORRESPONDENCE 13

AFFECTATIONS

Believe me, it gave me no pleasure to report your violation to Thief Squeak. I am assuming you are savvy enough to understand that I would personally be in violation for *not* reporting you, right? We pride ourselves in this corporation on the rugged independence of our employees, and so we must each look out for ourselves. Nobody holds your hand in The Corporation. We are developing hard and strong associates. You would not have been promoted if The Corporation didn't feel like you were up for the challenge.

I was saddened by your violation. Well, not so much in the violation itself, but that it represents a total lack of comprehension of all I have been teaching. You have to remember at all times: you are not immune to the enemy's devices. It is possible, very possible, to get sucked into the delusions the enemy fosters. You must constantly suppress your heart.

I've seen cold and ferocious sales associates, with great potential and inspiring ambition, fall tragically in love with their prospects. Seasoned associates, who marvel The Corporation with their malevolence, have crumbled into soft-hearted sobs, too weak and cowardly to proceed with their responsibilities. Some, even, have converted to the enemy's kingdom—and who knows what horrors they have endured *there*.

You must always be on guard. The path to failure starts with small, inconsequential steps—a little pity here, a little sentiment there. You must watch vigilantly for even the smallest traces of affection in yourself. Referring to your prospect by his name, as inconsequential as this may seem, can often be just intimate enough so as to open a door within yourself where the enemy can begin to stoke corrosive, counter-productive feelings of affection in you. This will not only ruin your chance at a sale, but can end your career in catastrophic fashion.

You must never refer to your prospect by his name. Is this clear, KX12? Don't even call him by a derogatory name (see statute 18,626.87c), because the enemy is masterful at turning even derogatory names into something that can trigger affection.

Of course, if it is someone else's prospect, call them whatever you want. But, to you, your own prospect is simply "prospect." Got it?

Remember, these rules are here for a reason. They are lessons born out of the struggles of war. They protect you and will help you succeed because in The Corporation we must always look out for one another. Keep up on your paperwork. Keep documenting. Keep a hard heart.

Sincerely,
Proktos Pew
Director of Information Dissemination and Outcomes Evaluation, Prospect Acquisition Department

CORRESPONDENCE 14

SELF-PITY

Recipient: KX12
Source: Proktos Pew
Transmission #00162
Prospect Age: 5y 5m 16days

Feeling pretty good about yourself, are you? I can practically feel your haughty eyes and arrogant sneer in your writing. You've zeroed in on that perfect emotion for your client: self-pity.

Big deal.

I practically held your hand the whole way to your little discovery (see Correspondence #00147).

Just so you know, none of us in management—those of us with names and titles—none of us are impressed. In fact, the savvy among us are laughing at you. You have no idea what you are getting yourself in to. You think because you found his precious emotion everything is going to be hot-sauce and relaxation. You're a fool.

You must learn that every opportunity is thick with risk. The enemy lurks around every corner. You must understand that the emotion most precious (and destructive) to your prospect is often related, due to yet another flaw in the enemy's design, to a corresponding strength. We've created a great variety of emotional products that are designed to exploit the destructive sides of these strengths, and to bend them to our own benefit. But those corresponding strengths, KX12 ...*yikes*! They are deadly.

Consider one of KX19's prospects, a girl who often doesn't get what she believes she deserves. Her skin gets red and her face crinkles. She's obviously angry, and she seems to get some cathartic pleasure from that anger. Novice tempters see this as free candy. But those of us who know what we are doing know that this anger might also be an expression of the girl's heightened sense of justice (even if her current, childish calculation of justice is flawed). In the hands of the wrong associate she could very well blossom into a powerful prophet! A warrior for social justice! An advocate for the underprivileged!

A prospect's preferred emotion often emerges from special gifts the enemy gives them. They're assets he implants for long term use. He wants the angry girl to invest her anger into constructive action. We simply want her to focus on the emotion itself, and, if possible, to have her get a sort of dark pleasure from it. Or, if that doesn't work, we want to offer her quick ways to expunge the anger. There is almost always a quick gain to every emotion that serves no ultimate purpose for the prospect. Look for those. Sell those.

Prospects seem overly thrilled by the gust of attention from others that an emotion can trigger. They love this. I might even claim attention as a prospect's *preferred* currency—at lease over the last hundred years or so. A little attention from others is often more rewarding to them than money, sex, or food. Can you believe that? We're not really even sure why—probably another flaw in the enemy's design—but they just really love attention. It's so funny how dumb they are. They have this cosmic power, this ability to drastically impact the world in the enemy's favor, but a shocking amount of the time they're satisfied with a little admiration, some show of pity, or a fleeting display of praise from their peers. This becomes delectably dis-empowering. I bet we've had a thousand celebrity prospects *raise awareness* for homelessness who have never developed any relationship with any actual homeless person.

Our self-pity products, you will find, are wonderfully compatible with all of our attention-seeking accessories. Tread lightly, though. Develop his self-pity, and his attention-seeking skills, gradually. The longer it takes the enemy to detect our play, the better. Although, once they're on to us, switch immediately to maximum intervention. Drench him in that self-pity product as thoroughly as you possibly can.

Onward!

Sincerely,

Proktos Pew

Director of Information Dissemination and Outcomes Evaluation, Prospect Acquisition Department

CORRESPONDENCE 15

SELECTIVE LISTENING

Recipient: KX12
Source: Proktos Pew
Transmission #00166
Prospect Age: 5y 6m 3days

Congratulations. You are finally caught up on your SCACs and PARs, but where, now, are your CATs [Counter-Authority Tactic Reports]? It's been several weeks! Remember, KX12, The Corporation is a data-driven organization. You know that, right? We need the facts.

It gives me little pleasure to say this, but you are a moron. I wouldn't say it if it were not true. Even a somewhat intelligent associate needs to rely on data. You… desperately so.

I saw you Tuesday evening jabbing him like a fool, trying to get him to throw a tantrum. Like many new associates, you get drunk on grandiose outbursts and explosions of disorderliness. You want fireworks and sensational happenings. Fun as that might be, it does little good for our campaign.

In fact, it merely distracts you from any real value-add opportunities. Take the Tuesday incident, for example. Your prospect was building some preposterous spaceship with his LEGO® blocks and mommy wanted him to come to the kitchen to eat. But your little space-architect wanted to finish his project and was not in the mood for dinner.

Mommy called for him and the prospect pretended not to hear her. She was frustrated, and so was he. She called again and prospect ignored it.

That's when you came stumbling in, trying to get him to destroy the neighborhood. You were stoking some real heated thoughts in that little blonde head of his, weren't you? But they were so heated that even he, a mere child, recognized them as utterly ridiculous. And he got right up and trotted into the dining room.

What a waste.

You thought the opportunity was a tantrum and ignored the far more profitable opportunity: his selective listening. It was right there in front of you, but you were too consumed in your own lust for chaos to see it. He was pretending not to hear mommy. The little snot was offering you pure gold, while you were hard-selling him for iron. Selective listening is a precious and lasting treasure. You should have been focusing all of your efforts on that.

Let me tell you a secret. Humans hate authority. They want to be able to do whatever they want, whenever they want. All by themselves, they construct strategies to counteract all authority. Selective listening is a glorious example of one of these early strategies.

Selective listening may look innocent, but it's not. This soft dismissal represents a fledgling challenge to authority. Our prospect lacks the wherewithal to challenge authority in a direct way, so he does so indirectly, by pretending not to hear. That way, if authority clamps down, he always has plausible escape. "I didn't hear you," he'll say (and how could she prove otherwise?).

What selective listening does is engage the prospect on an anti-authority journey that we can continue to nurture. It also forces the parent to react from their authority. It demarcates the relationship. Mommy escalates her tone. Or maybe even shouts. Maybe she uses fear. She reinforces authority as a scary, inhibiting force that overpowers. This all reinforces the prospect's disdain for authority and motivates him to seek more ways to counter it.

So, while a tantrum can be a great deal of fun, ultimately it is a mere party horn. A prospect's relationship with authority is the party itself.

When I was still a mere tempter, such as yourself, I once had a deaf prospect. Oh how I loved tormenting his father. Papa would try to give commands to my prospect, through sign language, but I had my prospect thoroughly trained to simply look away from papa at just that moment when papa was about to give important instruction. Then, when papa would scold my prospect for looking away, I'd have the boy look away from *that*. How amusing those fits of rage were from that silly father!

Any tempter can cause a toddler to throw a tantrum. But it takes a real skilled professional to work a toddler over so that he causes his mom or dad to tantrum.

Sincerely,
Proktos Pew
Director of Information Dissemination and Outcomes Evaluation, Prospect Acquisition Department

CORRESPONDENCE 16

THE BULLDOZER

Recipient: KX12
Source: Proktos Pew
Transmission #00192
Prospect Age: 5y 9m 8days

Buck up, KX12. This is the Prospect Acquisition Department, not the Grumble Department. You're simply feeling a bit overwhelmed. There is so much to consider. Your prospect is growing so fast with so many paths extending into his future. So many possibilities for him, and so many opportunities for you!

Be careful not to think too much at once. Narrow your focus. Prospects are won over by all the little things. Details, KX12. All the little details will drag the boy down.

In looking at your SAD [Social Adjustment Document] it seems you are, once again, failing to see the real opportunity in everyday situations. Take this scene, on page 13, from late last week when mother was trying to drop prospect off at his grandparent's house:

> "Prospect is mad at mom because he does not want to go to grandpa and grandma's house. But mom is forcing him to. I have been trying to stoke his anger. I've proposed some vicious thoughts about mother, but I can't seem to get prospect to elevate anger past an irrelevant point."

There are so many problems with your line of thought here. Where do I begin?

First, your report is terribly scant. *Tell me something*, KX12! Put some effort into it! Give me details! What was mother's expression? What was her mood? What was the weather like? Details, details, details!

Second, why all the effort into stoking his anger? I could have sworn we started him on a self-pity program? Trying to invoke his anger is bad marketing. We are sending him mixed messages. Should he feel anger or self-pity? If you are always lobbying for both, he'll feel neither—at least not in any useful amount. This is especially true with anger and self-pity. Self-pity is the morose acceptance of powerlessness. It reeks of smallness and harmlessness. Anger counteracts all of this! Anger is an inflamed sense of power. In fact, often, learning how to be angry liberates people entrenched in self-pity. So, for this boy, stick to the pity and keep him away from anger.

Remember, we are contending with a tireless enemy. There will be no low-hanging fruit. Once you begin a prospect on a program you must stay focused. Don't get distracted by cheap thrills and small acts of rage or destruction. Take the long-term approach, or you will fail.

Third, and you should feel embarrassed that I had to look at KX09's documentation since yours was so pathetic, you once again missed out on a golden opportunity. The real gem in this situation was mother's bulldozing behavior. KX09 has worked very hard on developing this habit in mom, and you are letting her hard work go wasted.

I'm assuming you realize that things are not going so well with mom and dad? Dad's been fired from his job, and mom's had to work extra hours. She's angry, exhausted, and brimming with dread about her marriage and her future. All she wants is some relief from her hassles so she can try to get some order in her life.

But the boy doesn't like to spend time at the grandparent's house. Who would? Grandma is an entitled gossip who spends every waking minute looking for flaws in people (to distract her from the catastrophe that is her own life, for sure), all while smoking two packs of cigarettes a day, filling the air with suffocating clouds of carcinogens. Grandpa is always nursing a low grade beer buzz and trying to stoke up self-righteous anger about how the president is destroying his country. They've cultivated a gloomy, uncomfortable environment nobody could enjoy, especially a small boy.

But the boy can't yet articulate this to mom. So he "puts up a fuss." Mom interprets this as mere childhood moodiness and bulldozes right over him, grabbing him by the forearm and dragging him into the smoke-infested house of disenchantment. This is where golden opportunity lies, KX12. Even a casual glance at the boy will show you the effectiveness of her bulldozing. Sure, he hollers and resists, but you'll also notice, past his feisty facade, undertones of abandonment and worthlessness. How could he interpret this hostile act as anything other than *I don't matter*, or, *I'm not important?*

Two little seeds of belief sprouted in his mind in that situation (which you failed to water): adults don't care, and communication is futile. Can't you see how wonderful this is? Tell me you can see the opportunity here! This is the birthplace of social apathy, KX12, and the soil is rich for this little boy.

Can you see, too, how all of this is more consistent with the work you are already doing within the self-pity program?

Sincerely,

Proktos Pew

Director of Information Dissemination and Outcomes Evaluation, Prospect Acquisition Department

CORRESPONDENCE 17

TURN SIGNALS

Recipient: KX12
Source: Proktos Pew
Transmission #00198
Prospect Age: 5y 11m 22days

I saw your PIMP [Playtime & Imagination Monitoring Protocol] and was alarmed. You note, with your typical lack of useful detail, that your prospect is engaging increasingly in abstract thought. On page 66:

> "Prospect has been playing with toys intended for older boys (soldiers and tanks and war planes). His play remains adequately violent, each episode with great imaginary casualty and destruction. However, he has had increasing episodes of daydreaming, where he seems to be engaging in abstract thought. There is no way for me to discern what he is thinking. I have no basis for speculation."

No basis for speculation? No way for you to discern? You have all kinds of evidence upon which you can speculate! You have the answer right in your PIDS [Playtime & Imagination Dictation Sheets]. Open your eyes, KX12. Put some effort into your work. Look on page 42, where he is playing with his soldier toys:

> …prospect then arranged a row of 12 enemy soldiers with their guns aimed at the protagonist, a lone soldier from the *good army* named Captain Perish.
> **Prospect's Narrator Voice:** "Surrounded by

Zorcon's evil troopers, and no more blasts in his blaster, what will Captain Perish do?"

Associate Comment 0114: Prospect stares at his little scene of toys, contemplating, I assume, an answer to his own narrative hook. After 2 minutes and 12 seconds, prospect animates one of the enemy soldiers and, in an enemy voice, says:

Enemy Soldier: "We've got you now, Captain Perish. Prepare for dying."

Captain Perish Voice: "Wait! Why do you want to kill me? What did I do?"

Enemy Soldier: "Zorcon commanded us to kill all those who are not with us. Those who fight Zorcon must be blasted to death! You must be blasted to death."

Captain Perish Voice: "Yeah, but do you really want to be on the same team as a jerk that kills everyone who think something different? What will he do to you if you ever think something different? He'll kill you, too, right? Why'd you be on that team?"

Associate Comment 0115: Prospect stared at his scene of toys for 4 minutes and 16 seconds, then:

Enemy Soldier: "Kill Captain Perish!"

Prospect's Narrator Voice: "But, just as the evil soldiers were putting their fingers on the triggers, there was a really bad earthquake, which shook the mountain to crumbles, crushing some soldiers, and blocking Captain Perish from the blasters. Perish ran over the mountain to his hideout...."

You've got the answer right there. You have to learn to see it. Look at Comment 0115, where the prospect has his longest reflective moment. Consider what is happening before and after this pause.

Remember, when a young prospect plays like this, the protagonist character, or the main toy, almost always represents the child in the child's mind. So, when Captain Perish asks the enemy soldier why he is a bad guy, this is something our prospect is asking. The long pause, then, happens because the boy doesn't have a good answer to his own question. He has no clue and, to our dismay, he devotes more and more time trying to figure it out.

Looking over your previous PIDS, it looks like his usual narrative includes an evil leader bent on world domination. But this narrative doesn't satisfy him anymore, does it? It is no longer plausible to him that Zorcon, if he were so evil, could get people to cooperate. Why would soldiers work with such an evil sob? Yes, of course there are reasons. But they remain too far beyond our boy's limited understanding and his lack of life experience for him to comprehend.

Most of these younger prospects are easy to manage because they are content with description. They only ask *that* questions. Most kids would be content with the proposition *that* Zorcon is evil, and *that* his soldiers are evil. Your little prospect is indeed demonstrating dangerous symptoms of abstract thought. He's beginning to look beyond *that* questions and is asking *how* and *why*. He's developing a faint hunger for understanding the way things really are

You have to understand a fundamental truth, which I call The Proktos Principle: *most people*

learn just enough to convince themselves they're right.
They learn just enough to reinforce their already
entrenched worldview. Typically, they embrace the
worldview of their parents, or of the dominant
culture, without reflection or critique. It is marvelous
how economical people can be when it comes to their
worldview!

Your prospect is becoming a bit of a thorn. If
symptoms of abstract thought persist, he will begin
to question everything on a deeper level and, once he
begins getting a handle on rational thought, we could
find ourselves at a significant disadvantage.

A foolish associate in this situation will try to
overpower his young intellect. My guess is that
you are already constructing eloquent arguments
to propose to him as to why a person would be a
bad guy. I bet you have a dozen explanations about
how an evil organization could inspire loyalty. This
is dumb. Don't waste your time with it. The better
approach is to find ways to smote his desire to use
abstract reasoning altogether. Leverage those closest
around him. Tap into their apathy and dysfunction.

In looking over this weekend's PILL (Parental
Interaction Log), I see opportunity everywhere. On
page 19 you record the boy asking mom: "If people
die in war, why do we have war?" To which mom
replied: "Nobody likes war, but sometimes people
disagree. Things get heated. Bad things happen."

"If nobody likes it and people die, why do it?"
"Because. It's just the way it is."
The boy continued asking *why* and mom

followed up wonderfully with a blizzard of dismissive proclamations: "It's the way it's always been," and, "It's a mystery," and, "Nobody knows." It's amazing how many ways humans have at their disposal to avoid saying, "I don't know." You see, if mother says, "I don't know," she is making a claim only about herself, and the boy is still at liberty to keep searching. But when she says, "It's a mystery," or, "Nobody knows," she is implying something more grandiose; namely, that trying to understand is futile. "It's a mystery," is a claim about greater reality. If it is a mystery, then there is no point in the boy pursuing the question. Do you see how suffocating this is to abstract thought?

Plus, mom is so tangle in her own inner realm. There's a thousand chunks of information about her own life she must attend to. There's her career, and all that new information she must learn about real estate investing. Then there's her decomposing relationship with her husband, and all of those argument fragments she is keeping in her active memory to use against him in case they should have another blow-up fight. She's got so much going on in that frazzled head of hers. It's a full-time job.

Take that frazzled head of hers and add our prospect asking, "Why?" over and over again like a swarm of angry hornets. Well, you get the idea. She loves the boy, of course, but just wants him to shut up.

You'll find the father will discourage the boy's abstract reasoning in a wholly different way. "Dad," he'll say, "why are there wars?" Dad will see this as an opportunity to "mess with the boy." Stubnugget has convinced dad that it is wonderfully funny to mislead the boy and get him to think absurd things. He'll say: "Wars happen when too many little boys disobey their parents." Or, remember when the boy asked him: "Are there any hurricanes named Hurricane Chase?" To which dad replied: "Of course not. That would be a *him*icane."

I once had a prospect who was anxious about using her turn signal. Why? Because her father once told her that if you leave the turn signal on too long the car will flip over. What a riot!

Dad's way of dealing with our prospect's abstract questioning, though less direct, is equally effective. The boy will quickly learn just how futile the pursuit of information is, and how it leads only to falsehoods and humiliation. He will abandon it altogether. Well, that is, if you do your job right.

Sincerely,
Proktos Pew
Director of Information Dissemination and Outcomes Evaluation, Prospect Acquisition Department

CORRESPONDENCE 18

A MAN'S MAN

Recipient: KX12
Source: Proktos Pew
Transmission #00237
Prospect Age: 6y 2m 26days

It looks like our prospect is beginning to mimic his father. Did you see how he rolled his eyes and contorted his face when mom told him to take his muddy shoes off Saturday? He made the same expression dad makes when the woman tells dad to do something. Or, do you see how he rests his hands in his back pockets in that same *cool guy* way dad does? Or how he sits on the couch watching cartoons with the same slothful slouch and smug indifference dad has when he watches his shows?

This is how I expected it to go. I anticipated him mimicking his dad more than his mom. Mom cares about our little chub's success and development, but her passion and intensity creates an unpleasant cloud of anxiety that turns everyone off. So, he has really begun gravitating towards dad, who is so easy to be around—a social perk of being a worthless oaf.

Plus, our prospect and his dad share the same gender, which biases him toward his dad to begin with—oh, this reminds me, he is entering this phase where he is beginning to understand his gender. This time in his life is rich with long-term opportunity. Our prospect is, biologically, a male. Obviously. But this biological classification is merely the basic level of his gender. The second level is how this biological reality plays out in the prospect's culture.

That is, what does it mean to be a male in life and in community. What does it *mean* to be a man? How he learns this, or rather, who he learns this from, is of utmost importance.

The third level of his gender, which we are still several years from focusing on, has to do with how his gender plays out sexually for him. You know, his sexual orientation, and other elements of his sexual persona. You may see subtle indicators, even now, revealing how this might play out for him. But they will be faint and infrequent (certainly watch for them, though, and document them when you see them).

For now we must focus on the second level. Go to your document repository and begin the GIJI (Gender Identity Journal Initiation Document). Consult with Stubnugget and KX09 to complete the sections on his parent's attitudes about gender. Though, for the sake of conversation, I can give you a good head start.

Mom and dad have totally different ideas about what it means to be a man. You see, mom wants our prospect to be a *good* man. She expects him to be honest, caring, helpful, and all that nonsense. She expects him to be a gentlemen. With little joy or celebration, she coaches him: "Keep negative opinions to yourself," and, "Be kind to strangers," and, "Always say please and thank you," and other inane commandments that she thinks are far more important than they really are. She's the kind of woman who can more easily forgive her son of robbery than for failing to hold the door open for a lady entering a convenience store.

Dad, on the other hand wants his boy to be a *real* man, which is wholly different than being a good man. Dad expects him to be tough, by which he means never showing emotion. He wants his boy to walk like a man, by which he envisions a strange mix of erectness and relaxedness, with an air of smug condescension (did you see how proud dad was when he saw the boy tie his boots? The boy, mimicking dad, lifted his foot up onto the truck bumper, adjusted the crotch of his pants, then tied his shoes. Dad was so proud. The elated goof had to suppress a tear!). Every time the boy does something mildly tough or manly, dad praises him with great pomp and circumstance.

To dad it's all about being a *man's man*. This vaguely means, to him, maintaining a fun-loving attitude and a constant glorification of masculinity. It means having the right attitude about men and the right attitude about women. In case you are not clear on the right attitude in question, it is an attitude that implies man's exulted status over women.

Indeed, pleasantly gullible prospects like dad are quick to discover that the fastest way to feel exulted is through belittlement. That's father through-and-through. In dad's mind, there exists a sharp distinction, a line in the sand, between men and women, and just watch how eager dad gets to make this difference known. Watch especially close when he is chumming around with his buddies. It is here that you can really see the gravitational dynamics of this adorably ridiculous behavior. When that line is drawn, there is an instant urge, an internal pull, in every male in the vicinity to be on the right side of that line. And, even more, to make it *known* to the other men that they are on the right side of that line (thereby, also, reinforcing the sacredness of the line).

His buddy Tripp made fun of Roger's "girly drink." And Roger, too, secured his masculinity later on when he commanded Tripp to "Stop crying like a woman." And did you hear that hilarious joke dad shared with them about the hot blonde on roller skates? Our prospect heard it. He has also heard dad chastise women drivers, and has seen how dad and his pals all look at women when they're around town. They gaze at them with the same predatory wonderment with which they stare at the burger menu. Those guys are a real riot, and our prospect already feels a strong pull deep in his little heart, a nascent appetite for their acceptance and approval.

All of this sends a clear message to the boy that dad, the man, is superior. And it all, of course, diminishes the boy's respect for mom and her authority. There is a new filter on the lens through which the boy interprets reality. How he looks at people, especially females, has become more nuanced. Watch for it. For instance, he has this new, subtle pause after everything mom says. A delay in his response. A dawdle in his obedience. Mom senses it, and recognizes the slight offense, but can't yet articulate exactly what it is.

This is all splendid. Totally splendid.
Onward!

Sincerely,

Proktos Pew

Director of Information Dissemination and Outcomes Evaluation,
Prospect Acquisition Department

CORRESPONDENCE 19

MR JIBBLES

Recipient: KX12
Source: Proktos Pew
Transmission #00238
Prospect Age: 6y 3m 0days

I am so furious with you right now I am tempted to demote you and finish converting your prospect myself! You're lucky I just returned from giving my seminar on The Proktos Principle. I'm exhausted.

Who is Mr. Jibbles? I had to look over KX09's KILLs [Kid Interaction Logs] to get the answer. In her charting I found this nauseating nugget:

> ...prospect and Chase were sitting barefoot on the back porch sharing slices of an apple. It was 90 degrees and they were, unfortunately, enjoying the sunshine. As they were eating together, with Chase leaning softly against prospect's shoulder, they saw an albino squirrel dashing through the grass and leaping up a maple tree.
> **Chase:** "Mom, look! There's that white squirrel again!"
> **Prospect:** "He's fast, isn't he?"
> **Chase:** "Yeah he is! Can I have another apple slice, please?"
> **Prospect:** "Yes you can. And you said please like a gentlemen. Good job!"
> **Chase:** "But why does he look like a marshmallow?"
> **Prospect**: "Some animals are like that. When they are white like that they are called albino. So that would be an albino squirrel."
> **Chase:** "Al-bino squirrel."
> **Associate Comment #0098:** Prospect is having a

truly joyful moment with her boy and all my efforts to sabotage have failed. At this point prospect is smiling more genuinely than she has in months. She puts an arm around her boy and says:

Prospect: "What name should we give him?"

Associate Comment #0090: Prospect's son seems especially intrigued with the notion of naming the squirrel. His expression is part joy, part concentration, and part exhilaration.

Chase: "How about… Mr. Jibbles?"

Associate Comment #0100: Prospect laughs and shake's her boys hand in a mock-formal ceremony and says:

Prospect: "Mr Jibbles it is. You are oh-so good at naming animals, Chase."

Bonding with his mom *and* with nature? Why didn't you mention any of this in your PILLs [Parental Interaction Logs]? And why was there no mention of *you* in KX09's very thorough documentation? Were you on holiday? Going for a walk, were you? You're fortunate KX09 didn't report you. If you can't handle the paperwork at this stage, KX12, you'll never survive when the boy gets to college.

If you had documented this failure I would've seen it and we could've done some contingency planning. But since you left it all undocumented, you set us up for yet another failure—which occurred this weekend. I mean, what the heaven were you thinking? You let your prospect wander into a crisis situation and failed to manage him effectively. The enemy crushed us, here, without even breaking a sweat.

It happened on Sunday while our little prospect and his dad were raking leaves. Here's your inadequate account of it from your most recent PILL, pages 96-97:

> ...prospect and his dad were raking leaves in the front yard, pulling the piles of leaves toward the street. There, near the curb, was a dead squirrel with its guts smushed out. Prospect became explosively emotional at the site of this and wept suddenly and violently. He yelled:
>
> **Prospect:** "Mr Jibbles!"
>
> **Associate Comment #0057:** Dad threw his rake and ran to the boy's side. His expression relaxed and he rolled his eyes when he saw it was just some dumb squirrel.
>
> **Dad:** "Chase, it's no big deal. It's just some dumb squirrel."
>
> **Prospect:** "It's Mr Jibbles," the boy exclaimed, through a snotty, tear-streaked face.
>
> **Associate Comment #0058:** Dad appeared to be embarrassed by prospect's crying and looked around at some neighbors. He shrugged toward them, then returned his attention to the boy. He then knelt down to prospect's level.
>
> **Dad:** "Chase, buddy, calm down. Hey, the squirrel is only sleeping. He's taking a nap."
>
> **Prospect:** "No he's not!"
>
> **Associate Comment #0058:** Prospect ran away from dad, tripped on a rake, fell face-first into the freshly raked grass, got up, then ran in to the house, weeping louder and louder as he ran...

It wasn't "just a dumb squirrel" to the boy, you

fool. He was Mr Jibbles. He was the white squirrel who the boy gave a name to. He was special. He was the boy's strange little outdoor friend. The boy's father (and more importantly, *you*) didn't understand this. So our prospect went on a desperate journey for someone who would understand: Mom. You pick up the scene on page 99:

...prospect's mom was studying real estate books at the kitchen table when she heard prospect running through the kitchen crying. She got up and prospect jumped into her arms, and she lifted him up to her shoulder. Prospect wept into mom's shoulder while mom caressed the boy's back.

Mom: "Chase, what happened? Are you okay?"

Prospect: "Mr Jibbles," he began, but couldn't stammer much more through the tumult of his weeping. He merely pointed toward the outside and said, "in the street."

Associate Comment #0060: The boy buried his face again in mom's shoulder.

Prospect's Mom: "Oh, poor Mr Jibbles," she said, and patted prospect's back with disgusting affection. When prospect's weeping lessened, she sat with him on her knee and said, while looking him in the eyes, "Mr Jibbles was a great squirrel, wasn't he?" While prospect was nodding, she continued. "He would be so happy to know that a great little boy like you was sad that he died. And, you know what? How many squirrels have a great name like Mr Jibbles?" Prospect sniffled and continued nodding. With some apprehension and uncertainty, she continued: "Hey. Let's go give Mr Jibbles a proper burial. What do you think?"

Associate Comment #0061: Prospect and mom

then went out and buried the squirrel by the shed.

Went out and buried him by the shed, huh? You thought that adequately documented the event, did you? Well, KX09 seems to have a better comprehension of what is important. In looking over her report she notes many important elements from that impromptu burial ceremony that you seemed to not think much of.

First, our prospect *prayed*. How did you not think this was important to document? My eyes burned when I read it in KX09's documentation, but there it was. After digging the hole, putting the shoebox coffin in, and covering it with dirt, mom said a prayer. Then your prospect, who you are trying to convert, said a prayer! *"God, thank you for Mr Jibbles. Thank you for mom. Tell Mr Jibbles his name for me and that mom and I will see him in heaven. Amen."*

Not only did you not document this crucial incident in your PILL [Parental Interaction Logs], but you also failed to fill out the F-PED [First Prayer Experience Document].

Second, and almost as important, we have squandered a whole lot of great progress we were making on his gender development. Look how far along he was with modeling his view of his gender off of the hilarious template of his father. We had him set up so we could, for years to come, push him around with his own masculinity. Now that is wrecked and must be rebuilt. Dad's machismo was a complete turn-off to the boy and you let him run and find comfort with his mom, thereby indirectly affirming her ideology and discrediting dad's.

I mean, how could you be so stupid? You should've never even let him see the squirrel. You allowed this situation to devolve in to utter failure.

Don't get me wrong. His gender identity can be rebuilt. There are still fragments of that old gender ideology in that little head of his. KX09 noted that dad saw the little ceremony between our prospect and mom, and that dad rolled his eyes and made a scoff noise, which your prospect noticed. She further noted that the boy still looks like he has some shame about not being a *real man*. We can work with that. But it's all rework. We could have been pushing him on to other things by now.

I am issuing an order for you to read Grandmaster FesterLump's six-volume series on gender identity manipulation. I expect a completed RIP [Reading Integration Plan] on my desk by next Tuesday.

Sincerely,
Proktos Pew
Director of Information Dissemination and Outcomes Evaluation, Prospect Acquisition Department

CORRESPONDENCE 20

GABBY HAND

Recipient: KX12
Source: Proktos Pew
Transmission #00249
Prospect Age: 6y 3m 20days

Thank you for your comments about my most recent paper: "Understanding and Leveraging the Proktos Principle in Prospect Conversion Strategy." Good news! The Corporation has decided to publish it in *The Journal of Prospect Acquisition*. I'll be sure to send you a signed copy as soon as it comes out.

So, mom and dad are going out on a date. My sources tell me they are going on this date in a desperate attempt to rekindle romance in their slowly dying marriage.

The important thing for our purposes, right now, is not their inevitable divorce, but, rather, who our prospect's babysitter will be.

There are currently two candidates:

The first is Samantha Goodwin. She is 15 and already more entrenched in the enemy's camp than most church leaders. Her gushing affection and steadfast compassion stinks up the room, and her devotion to the christ, naive as it may be, is genuine and impenetrable. She is out of your league, KX12, and could unleash disastrous influence on our budding chub. KX23 is her associate in The Corporation, and is in totally over his head. Samantha, and the enemy, have bested KX23 at every point.

I'm far more intrigued by the other candidate.

Gabriel ("Gabby") Hand is 14 years old. He is managed masterfully by FlopSweat. The little chump is a budding sexual predator. Basically abandoned by his parents' monstrous obsession with their careers, little Gabby spends many hours channeling his isolation and bitter feelings into dark pornography. The boy has been equipped with a dazzling imagination, which he squanders on wonderfully dumb little scenes of sexual conquest—conquests of the deliciously destructive sort. He hasn't fondled any children yet, but FlopSweat tells me it's only a matter of time. And our little prospect would be a fantastic candidate for him to finally make some of his dark little dreams real.

Now, KX12, remember when I told you that other people can penetrate our little prospect's cloud of innocence? It just so happens that Samantha is unavailable to babysit Saturday night. Sshe will be at some Urban Outreach event sharing the enemy's propaganda with a bunch of drunk homeless men.

So, Samantha Goodwin is busy Saturday Night. But Gabby Hand has no other plans and is sincerely excited to get to know our little prospect.

Onward!

Sincerely,

Proktos Pew

Director of Information Dissemination and Outcomes Evaluation, Prospect Acquisition Department

TO BE CONTINUED...

For a FREE study guide to Volume One,
and to be alerted immediately
when Volume Two is complete, go to:

www.KX12Book.com

You can also follow Dan at:
twitter.com/thatdankent

And Proktos has been discovered at:
twitter.com/ProktosPew

More Books by Dan Kent:

**The Training of KX12:
Volume Two**

**The Training of KX12:
Volume Three**
(coming soon)

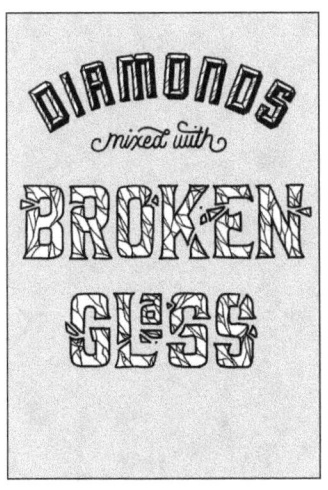

**Diamonds Mixed with
Broken Glass**

Confident Humility:
Becoming Your Full Self without
Becoming Full of Yourself

Hello. What are you still doing here? The book is done for now. Come back in Volume Two.

Well, since you're here, what did you think of this first volume? I'd love to hear your thoughts. Hit me up on Twitter (@thatdankent), or drop me a comment on Facebook: Facebook.com/ trainingKX12.

Thank you SO much for reading my work.